W9-BGK-167

This 2004 edition published in the U.S. by

Backpack Books
Backpack Books, Inc., 122 Fifth Ave,
New York, NY 10011

First published in Great Britain in 2004 by
Gullane Children's Books, an imprint of Pinwheel Limited,
Winchester House, 259-269 Old Marylebone Road, London NW1 5XJ

1 3 5 7 9 10 8 6 4 2

Giselle, Swan Lake, Sleeping Beauty, and *The Nutcracker*
(previously published in the UK as individual titles)
Text © Adèle Geras 2000
Illustrations © Emma Chichester Clarke 2000

Coppélia and *The Firebird*
Text © Adèle Geras 2004
Illustrations © Emma Chichester Clarke 2004

ISBN 0-7607-5989-8

Printed and bound in China

ADÈLE GERAS & EMMA CHICHESTER CLARK

My First
Ballet Stories

BACK**PACK**BOOKS

∘

NEW YORK

Cont

ents

The Magic of the Ballet

HUMAN BEINGS LIKE TO move their bodies in time to rhythm. Even the tiniest babies enjoy being rocked or gently bounced as you sing to them, and we all know how feet long to move when we hear a strong and exciting beat. "That's toe-tapping music," we say, and what we mean is we would like to dance to it.

There are many different kinds of dancing: folk, ballroom, tap, and so on.

Classical ballet is dancing that follows a very particular set of rules, and some of these go back to the seventeenth century, when such dancing was first seen as a short interlude in the middle of a play, a pleasant break from lines and lines of dialogue. Because there are no spoken words on stage, the same ballets are understood in any country.

The stories behind the ballets are tales of love and transformation, of death and ghosts, of lakes and dark forests and strange creatures. As the curtains open on a ballet, we become part of a magical world and share all its enchantments. We marvel at the grace and discipline of the dancers; at the beauty they create.

"It was Giselle's voice, and I was filled with
a happiness I thought was lost forever."

Giselle

EVERYTHING THEY SAY ABOUT old age is true. I find that I remember in the clearest detail everything that happened to me in my youth, and yet I would have difficulty in telling you what I ate this morning when I awoke.

Sometimes I forget how quickly the years have gone by, and, when I catch sight of myself in the glass, I do not recognize the white-haired old man I see. This cannot be me, Albrecht. Albrecht was tall and straight. He had clear blue eyes and a smiling mouth. And he was loved, oh, yes indeed. I may have forgotten many things, but the memory of Giselle's love for me still remains. I think of her every day, and there is a small, vain part of my soul that rejoices to think she never saw me as an old man. To her, I am still young.

Giselle lived in the village of . . . but no, the name has gone. No matter. It was a collection of small, well-kept cottages that clung to the side of a hill where the forest ended.

I was hiding in this village, I confess it. I had become bored with palace life, with ceremony, with decorum, and all I wanted that spring was to roam through the woods like a peasant, hunting when it suited me.

It wasn't really even Bathilde that I was escaping from. Our families had arranged for us to be married. Bathilde was considered to be a beauty, and her father was the Duke of Courland. My parents persuaded me that it would be a splendid alliance, and I reluctantly agreed. My flight to the village was a last chance for the kind of freedom I knew I could never have as a married man, nor as the future Duke of Silesia.

If it were not for Giselle, I probably would have returned to the palace within days, but, once I caught sight of her, everything else in my life shrank away, and I never gave the palace or my duty a single thought. I found a cottage and paid the owner money to rent it, and I took the name of Loys.

How can I find words to describe Giselle? I loved her from the very first moment I laid eyes on her, and she loved me, too. She was pale. Her hair was like ravens' feathers. She danced for happiness, but there was always something fragile about her. I don't know how to put it more accurately. Always I had the thought in my mind when we were together: "Be careful, oh, be careful,"—for I knew she could so easily be hurt.

Hilarion, the young gamekeeper in the village, adored Giselle, too. He could see that Giselle and I loved each other, and his jealousy grew and grew.

On the morning of the harvest feast, I came very near to telling Giselle who I really was.

She had been teasing me, asking me why it was that I was different from other men she had known and begging me to tell her where I had come from and who my family were.

"It doesn't matter," I answered. "You are my family, my whole world. You are the one I love."

"Oh, but do you? Do you truly? Let this flower tell us." She picked a late rose and began idly to pluck the petals from it. "He loves me, he loves me not. . . . "

"Will you believe a flower that knows nothing of how I feel? Will you not believe me?"

Suddenly I was filled with dread at what Giselle would do if the last petal fell on "he loves me not." How relieved I was then, to pull the last petal from the stem.

"I love you! You see? Even this rose knows this is the truth!" I cried.

Giselle smiled, happy for the moment.

"Go with the others, Loys, to gather the last of the harvest, and I will stay here and prepare the feast," she said.

And I went. I went gladly. I thought myself the most fortunate man alive, striding away with the others into the valley while the September sun shone all around us, as golden and sparkling as the wine we would soon be enjoying. Try to imagine my joy as a bubble, and look at it now, catching the light. Soon it will burst, and neither I nor anyone else will ever lay eyes on it again.

Much later, during that long, infinitely black night, while we watched over Giselle's body before her funeral, her weeping mother told me what had happened. I hear her words even now, half a lifetime later. I still wonder if there was anything I could have done differently that would have prevented Giselle's dreadful end.

"We heard the horns, and the hounds baying," her mother told me, "and soon a hunting party arrived in the village. Everyone gathered around, for we had never seen such grand people. Princess Bathilde was the most splendid of all, in a gown the color of a dark red rose. Everyone rushed forward, offering hospitality. Giselle helped to serve the wine, and Princess Bathilde was struck by her beauty and grace."

Here Giselle's mother paused and wiped the tears from her eyes. "Bathilde asked my poor daughter question after question. She begged her to come to the palace as her own serving lady, but, when she found out that Giselle was in love and soon to be married, she smiled kindly.

"'It is my loss,' she said, 'and you shall have my own necklace as a wedding gift.'

"She fastened a chain of gold filigree around Giselle's neck, and my daughter danced away to show the wonderful present to all her friends. The royal party came into my house to rest

before their homeward journey, and then you came back from the vineyards, and the festival began. My daughter had been chosen as the Queen of the Harvest. How joyously she danced! Do you remember? Oh, oh, I cannot bear to think of what has happened!"

And I, even though I cannot bear it, am condemned to turn it over constantly in my mind. I remember how we danced and then how Hilarion came rushing from my cottage brandishing my sword. Wine had given Hilarion courage. He parted us, Giselle and me, by placing the blade between us, and his face was twisted with hatred.

"You are the son of the Duke of Silesia, and not Loys at all. I have the proof." He turned to the villagers. "He brought too many possessions with him for a humble peasant. He has deceived us, and he has bewitched you, Giselle, with his false promises."

The royal party came out of Giselle's cottage to see what all the shouting was about, and Bathilde caught sight of me at once.

"Albrecht!" she cried. "What are you doing here among these simple folk?" She ran to my side and said, "See, Giselle? I, too, have my betrothed. This is Albrecht, and I hope that you will be as happy in your marriage as we in ours." Each word was like a dagger in my poor Giselle's heart! Giselle turned to me.

"Please say that she is lying, Loys," she whispered. My mouth was full of ashes, and my heart was as cold as a stone in my body. I could say nothing.

Do you believe that someone can die of a broken heart? I had thought it was a fanciful notion, invented by lovesick poets, but that was before Giselle's death.

She tore at the necklace Bathilde had given her, and it snapped as if it were no more than a thin string of silk. Then she took my jeweled sword from Hilarion and plunged it into her side. How could he have let her take it? How could he have prevented her? She had the strength of despair in her hands. Still, it was not the wound that killed her. I did. I killed her as surely as if I had squeezed the life out of her with my own hands. She danced like a marionette with broken strings. She danced like a doll with no life left in her. Her soul flew out of her before our eyes. The anguish in her heart drove all reason from her, and she fell at last into her mother's arms.

The feast was over. No one moved for a long time. Then Bathilde's party left the village. There was nothing they could do. No one was interested in them anymore. We were numb with grief, all of us, and hardly noticed the departure. There was nothing left for us to do but mourn.

"I should throw you from this house," said Giselle's mother, "but my daughter loved you." That was how I came to watch all night over Giselle's body, until her funeral the next day.

Do you believe in Wilis? They are the spirits of young girls who have died before their wedding day, deceived by their lovers, tricked by lies. There were tales told about them by country people. It was said that they appeared at midnight on the swampy shores of a hidden lake, led by their queen, Myrtha, who was tall and white and merciless. The Wilis danced till the first light of dawn, and, as the sun's rays touched them, they dissolved, every one of them, into thin mists, stretching and curling and hovering over the water. If an unfortunate young man were to meet one of them in the dark, he would be enchanted by her beauty and she would dance with him, in and out of the black trees in the moonlight, and her white, white arms would wind themselves like smoke around his neck, and she would call to her sisters, and together they would come and follow the dance, until there was no more strength in him and he breathed his last.

Everyone warned me. "Do not go to Giselle's grave at night. Some say she is now one of Queen Myrtha's misty maidens, and she will dance you to your death."

But I thought, "If I could see Giselle again, I would gladly pay with my life." So I said only, "There are flowers I must lay on her grave. Do not try to prevent me." I knew that there was no one brave enough to stop me as I made my way to where she lay buried.

I threw myself down near the wooden cross carved with Giselle's name. I was beside myself with grief. Then I saw Hilarion slipping through the trees. Could he have arrived before me? The thought flew in and out of my mind like a butterfly, and waves of sorrow overwhelmed me. I laid my face on the cold earth.

"My darling," said a voice near me, and I knew it. It was Giselle's voice, and I was filled

with a happiness I thought was lost forever. I looked up, and the blood froze in my veins. It was indeed Giselle, and yet she was transformed. Her eyes were like black pools, and her mouth was a bloodstain in her chalk-white face.

"Go, my love," she whispered. "I cannot protect you from your fate if you remain here. They . . . we will surely lead you to your grim death. Come quickly with me, and I will endeavor to hide you."

I followed her into the darkness between the trees, but at that moment we saw Hilarion dancing with the white maidens. I watched him, pulled this way and that like something blown by the wind or pulled by the tides, until at last he sank into the waters of the black lake whose surface glittered in the moonlight.

"Look," Giselle whispered. "Our queen approaches." Queen Myrtha towered over her maidens. Her face was a mask, and her dress moved around her like a cloud.

"There is a stranger in our midst," she said. "I can smell him. Giselle, where have you hidden him, the man who drove you to your death? Bring him out to us. We wish for him to dance with us."

Giselle turned to me. "Hold tightly to the cross on my grave," she said. "It is the only thing that will protect you. Do not let go.

Whatever happens, hold tightly onto the cross. I will plead with our queen. Perhaps she will be merciful."

Giselle begged for my life, but Queen Myrtha was unmoved.

"He will dance," she said, "like all the others. He will dance until he can dance no longer. Go to him."

At first, I shut my eyes and clung to the cross, but I couldn't bear not to see my beloved when she was so close to me.

"Turn away," she cried. "Hold fast."

But I could not. I had to hold her in my arms once more. I had to dance with her, even if death was the punishment.

"No," she whispered. "How will I protect you if they come . . . all my pale sisters?"

And of course they did come, all the ghostly dancers, pulling me here and there, making me feel dizzy and sick.

"Do not fall, my love," Giselle said to me as

we whirled and turned. "Lean on me. I will carry you. Do not lose heart. The light of dawn will soon be here."

As we danced, I lost all thought of where I was, and yet I knew that the Wilis were drawing me closer and closer to the water. Sometimes I caught sight of it among the trees but only for an instant, so frantic was the dance. I could feel Giselle breathing cold words of love in my ear.

"Come with me. The dawn is nearly here."

Blindly, nearly exhausted, I followed her. We were very near her grave. I could see the cross I should have clung to and my own flowers beside it. Then, I caught sight of the sky above the trees. Day was breaking.

"Thank the Lord," Giselle said, "for another dawn. They cannot touch you now. Look."

The Wilis were melting in the light. Even their queen was blurring at the edges and fading away among the trees.

"Stay," I groaned. "Do not leave me here alone, Giselle. What will I do but weep for you?"

"Then weep you shall," she sighed, "for I must return to the grave."

Her shape was disappearing into the earth. Before I could say another word, she was gone. She had saved me with her love and condemned me to a lifetime of remorse and sorrow.

That life is now almost at an end. I pray that beyond the grave I will be reunited with Giselle. I pray for that.

*"There was the 'niece,' the beautiful young lady
I had seen sitting on a chair on the balcony."*

Coppélia

THE CELEBRATIONS ARE OVER. The splendid new bell has been hung in the church, and its silver voice sings out over the rooftops, calling the people to prayer. Franz and I are officially engaged. Dr. Coppélius has been given a sum of money to repair anything in his house that needs repairing and also as a kind of apology from the town.

I suppose I am the chief cause of any unhappiness the poor doctor feels, and for that I am most sincerely sorry. My deception seemed like such harmless fun when I thought of it, and, in any case, let us not forget what he did to poor Franz. Let me tell you what happened, and you will judge for yourself.

My name is Swanilda. I have lived in this town all my life, and, for as long as anyone can remember, the tall black house on the market square has belonged to Dr. Coppélius. My grandmother tells me that even in her childhood he never invited anyone into it, nor did he open the windows to let in the daylight. Dr. Coppélius must be very old, but he has never looked different from the way he is now. Perhaps he was born gray-haired and stooped and as thin as a skeleton. He makes toys and sells them in the market. There's not a child in the town who has not played with one of his carved dolls or hobby horses or jack-in-the-boxes. You would have thought that such a toymaker would be loved by every child for miles around, but Dr. Coppélius was feared by the little ones and ridiculed by the swaggering young men who had grown up on stories of the dark deeds that (according to their nursemaids) took place in the shadowy rooms of the house whose shutters were always closed.

Imagine my astonishment then, when, a few days ago, I saw a most beautiful young lady sitting quite openly on Dr. Coppélius's balcony, reading a book.

"Look!" I said to my friends. "That's the first time anyone has ever visited Dr. Coppélius. Maybe she's a relative of his."

I called up to her in a friendly sort of way, but she didn't even look at me. I thought she was proud and stuck-up and decided to leave her reading, if that was what she enjoyed. When I caught a glimpse of Franz coming into the square, I hid myself at once. I knew he was going to flirt with this total stranger on Dr. Coppélius's balcony, and that was exactly what he did. I watched him doing it.

It's not that I am especially jealous by nature, just that Franz and I had already decided that we would be married. We had been close friends since we were small children, and I loved him dearly. Until I saw him talking to this silent young woman, I would have said he loved me. I gave him a piece of my mind, you may be sure.

"But I was only being friendly," he said. "Aren't you even a little bit curious to know who this young lady is? How often have you seen a visitor in that house?"

"Nevertheless," I sniffed. "There's friendliness and friendliness. You were not using the words you would use if you were addressing a toothless old crone. I know you too well, Franz. You think she is prettier than I am.

I don't know if I'm ready to marry someone who is so fickle."

Just then, Dr. Coppélius appeared on the balcony, and, together, he and the young woman made their way back into the dark house. Franz went about his business, still protesting his undying love for me, and I decided to wait in the square to see what would happen next. Some of my friends were with me. We saw the door of Dr. Coppélius's house open, and the old toymaker himself shuffled out, blinking, a little unaccustomed to the bright sunlight. He turned out of the square and made his way down a small cobblestone street.

"He dropped his key on the ground, look!" I said to my friends. "Let's go in and talk to the niece or whoever she may be. No one has ever been into that house. Just think what stories we'll be able to tell. Will you come with me?"

Such terrible tales were told about the doctor's magic powers that they were afraid at first, but I persuaded them in the end.

"What possible magic can he work," I said, "if he's not even here in the house?"

At last, they agreed to come with me, and we all tiptoed as quietly as we possibly could through the black door. We made our way along gloomy corridors, trying to keep our spirits up by giggling and holding hands. There was no sign of the pretty girl, and, even though we called out to her as we walked through the house and up the stairs, only silence answered us, a silence so deep that it rang in our ears.

When we reached the upper floor, we found the toymaker's studio. Even I, who had been pretending not to be the least bit scared, found this room to be a little upsetting. This was the place where Dr. Coppélius made his dolls. There were arms and legs hanging from hooks, and blank-faced bald heads propped up on sticks, waiting for wigs. There were glass balls painted to look like real eyes, lying in a tray on one table, and, worst of all, there were the finished dolls, who were sitting around the workshop, looking at us through their staring, enameled eyes.

"He is certainly very skillful," said my friend Maria. "Look at that mandarin over there and the knight on his horse."

"I like these two life-sized monkeys in pink

brocade," I said, "and this pretty Spanish dancer. But where is Dr. Coppélius's niece?"

"She's not here," said Maria. "Don't you think we'd better go? What if the doctor comes back and finds us?"

"First just let me see what's in this cupboard," I said.

"What if it's locked?" Maria whispered.

It was not locked. When I opened it, there was the 'niece', the beautiful young lady I had seen sitting on a chair on the balcony. I burst out laughing.

"Franz has been flirting with a doll!" I cried. "Oh, he is bound to feel like such a fool when I tell him. Dr. Coppélius has tricked us all. He has made a doll so perfect that we all thought she was alive."

I don't know who it was that managed to set the clockwork (or magic, or whatever it was) in motion, but suddenly the whole room was filled with Dr. Coppélius's creatures going through their mechanical paces.

"How clever they are!" cried my friends, but I was too busy examining the doll I had found to look at the other toys.

Truly, she was a thing of beauty. I imagined Dr. Coppélius working through the long, quiet nights, putting her still limbs together, carefully mixing his paints to the exact color of flesh that matched my own, sticking down each lock of the hair that was so like mine, touching her long eyelashes with soft brushstrokes. It was easy to see that this was a labor of love.

"We could be sisters," I whispered to her.

Then, all at once, there was the doctor,
shouting at us, flapping his cloak in all
directions. My friends were screeching and
crying and running around the room and out
of the door and down the stairs as fast as their
legs could carry them. No one stopped for me,
but I was near the cupboard. I didn't think. I
simply locked myself in with the doll and
listened as Dr. Coppélius soothed his toys,
winding them down, stopping their constant
movement as gently as any caring father, while
he tidied up the room. I hid and waited for a
chance to escape, and then I thought of a
clever trick I could play on the good doctor.

Quickly, I undressed the doll, took off my
own clothes, and put hers on instead. Then
I hid her limp, white body at the back of
the cupboard and sat down in her chair,
pretending to read her book. I knew it would
not be too long before the doctor came to

make sure that no harm had come to his most treasured creation.

"There you are, my darling," he crooned. "Safe and untouched. I don't think I could have borne it if any of those silly young girls had harmed you."

Just then there came a tapping at the window. Dr. Coppélius turned to see who it was, but I had already spotted Franz, who had clearly climbed a ladder to catch sight of the pretty stranger once more. What a surprise there was in store for him! Dr. Coppélius half-closed the cupboard door, and went to the window.

"Welcome, dear sir," he said. "I assume you have come to visit me, even though you have chosen a somewhat unusual way to enter the house. Surely it would have been far easier for you to knock at the door."

Franz climbed into the room, looking uncomfortable. "I'm sorry, Dr. Coppélius," he said. "It's just that the young lady . . . well, I did want to see her again and assure her of my friendship."

"Certainly, young man, certainly," said Dr. Coppélius. "See her you will, but first of all, have a glass of wine with me."

I should have declared myself then, and Franz and I should have run out into the square together, but I was jealous. Franz, it seemed, was interested enough in the young lady to risk breaking into someone's house. I told myself I didn't care what happened to him, but I was wrong. In a few minutes, it became clear that the wine had been drugged and the doctor was laying my poor Franz out on a table. Then he came and spoke to me.

"There, Coppélia dear. I have drugged him. Now I will use my best magic to transfer his life force into you."

Of course, I never really believed in any of it: all that nonsense with the spells and the smoke and the way Dr. Coppélius waved his bony fingers in the air and hummed to himself . . . and yet, the dolls in his workshop *did* all move in a most intriguing manner. Had they, too, been enchanted? Was it possible? I knew at once what I had to do. My task was to distract him from Franz, and I knew exactly how to do it, too. I would come to life, but little by little, and he would be so overwhelmed with his own brilliance in creating such a marvel that he would leave poor Franz alone.

My trick worked better than I could have hoped. From jerky, wooden movements, I progressed very speedily into such natural gestures that soon I was able to walk around the room quite freely.

"Oh, my beloved Coppélia!" cried the doctor. "You are wondrous beyond anything I have ever imagined! How full of love I am for you! Dance for me, my beauty. Dance!"

And so I did dance. I danced a Spanish dance and a Scottish dance, and Dr. Coppélius was beside himself with joy.

Whenever the doctor wasn't looking, I ran to Franz and shook him and spoke into his ear, and, at last, after what seemed like hours to me, he began to stir. I seized my opportunity. I spoke.

"Dr. Coppélius, I have to tell you the truth. My name is not Coppélia. It is Swanilda.

Your doll is still lying in the cupboard. I have played a trick on you, and I'm sorry, but this young man is my betrothed, and, when I saw that you had drugged him, I was frightened of what you might do to him."

Dr. Coppélius gave a cry of horror and rushed to the cupboard. I thought he would shout at us or threaten us in some way or chase us from his house, but his thoughts were centered on Coppélia. He carried her floppy white body in his arms and sank to the ground, weeping.

"Come," said Franz. "Let us go while he isn't looking."

I went with Franz, but I haven't been able to forget the sight: poor, thin, gray Dr. Coppélius embracing a lifeless bundle of cloth and stuffing and paint in the half-light of the workshop. I could hear him moaning as we left. "I thought you had come to life, my darling. I thought you could dance for me forever. How will I manage now? What will I do?"

The next day was filled with joy and sunshine and feasting. Franz and I agreed to become formally engaged, and we received a handsome dowry from the mayor of the town. I suppose no real harm was done, but I for one will no longer join in any gossip about Dr. Coppélius. I feel sorry for him because, even though he has been compensated for the damage we did in his house, all the money in the world will never buy him a living companion, and loneliness must be the iciest of sorrows. I am the only person in the town who truly knows Dr. Coppélius because I was his Coppélia for a while, and I felt the warmth and tenderness of his love.

"Von Rothbart swooped down from his branch, and the black span of his wings obscured the moon."

Swan Lake

LISTEN. THESE THINGS HAPPENED long ago. There was daylight and darkness. There was Good and Evil. There was the kingdom and the forest. In the kingdom, Prince Siegfried was about to celebrate his birthday. The forest, however, was the lair of the magician Von Rothbart.

In the deepest and greenest part of the forest, there was a silver lake that people called "The Lake of Swans." Whispers were that every bird floating on the still waters was really a young maiden trapped by Von Rothbart and transformed into a swan for as long as there was light in the sky.

At dusk (so the story went), each bird took on her human shape for the length of the night, and, in this way, Von Rothbart would remind them of the human happiness they had lost. Every single night, the magician took on the feathers and talons and wide, amber eyes of an enormous owl, and he sat and watched the pale dancers from the branches of a tree beside the lake. The most magnificent swan of all was once a princess. As the sun set, and her feathered wings fluttered into arms, she would remember her name.

"I was Odette," she would sigh. "Once, I was Odette."

But listen. It was the day of Prince Siegfried's birthday, and, in the palace, everyone was preparing for the celebrations.

The Queen had planned a ball, and every eligible young lady from every neighboring country had been invited.

"It is time," the Queen told her son, "that you found yourself a wife. There is a limit to the time a young man of royal birth should spend in frivolous pursuits such as hunting."

"Then why, dearest Mother, did you present me with this crossbow as a birthday gift?" replied the Prince.

"Because I knew it would please you," said the Queen. "In return, I insist that you please me and choose a wife at the ball tomorrow night."

"Very well, Mother," said Prince Siegfried. "You know I would do anything to bring a smile to your lips. Until the ball, however, I am a free man, and I'll enjoy my "frivolous pursuits," as you call them, for a little while longer."

Siegfried looked out of the window, thinking that maybe it was too late to go hunting that day. Just then, however, a formation of white swans crossed the sky, flying towards the dense forest.

"Come," Siegfried called to his companions, "we may be too late, but how beautiful they are! Let's follow them."

The hunting party set off. Although the young men had heard stories about the foolishness of wandering through the forest at dusk, they put them out of their minds. Were they not armed? And what royal prince would ever admit that he was afraid? Nevertheless, as the shadows thickened and the sky grew dark, Prince Siegfried's friends urged him to return to the safety of the palace.

"Wait," said Siegfried. "Can you see something white moving through the branches? I'm going to look."

He arrived at the clearing beside the lake in time to watch the great, white birds that he had been hunting fly down to the ground. He raised his crossbow to his shoulder and aimed it at the most glorious swan of all, when suddenly, in a shudder of white light, the wings bent themselves into arms, the pale feathers were gone, and his arrow was pointed at the loveliest woman he had ever seen. The other birds had also turned into young maidens, but Siegfried threw down his bow and ran towards the one he already knew he would love forever.

"Please," he implored, as she tried to escape him. "Please, I will never hurt you, I promise. Please do not run from me."

In his nearby tree, Von Rothbart, in the guise of an owl, hooted and spread his dark wings, but Siegfried had eyes and ears only for the woman before him.

When he caught up with her, she

trembled in his arms as though she were still a bird and he a hunter, but his kind words soothed her at last, and she spoke her name aloud to him.

"I am the Princess Odette," she said, "and I am condemned to be a swan during the daylight hours. We are all in Von Rothbart's power, and at night we dance in human form, but he watches us always. Even now, his eyes are fixed on us."

"Where?" cried Siegfried. "Show him to me, and I will put a single arrow through his heart."

"Oh, no, you must not," cried Odette, "or else you will surely kill me! He has bound his life to mine and twisted them together in a single thread. If he dies, then so will I. The spell will be broken only when I can find the person who will love me forever—someone who will be faithful to me alone."

"Then you are free," Siegfried laughed, "because I will love you through this life and beyond it. Come with me, and be my bride."

Hearing these words, Von Rothbart swooped down from his branch, and the black span of his wings obscured the moon. He clawed Odette to his side.

"Go!" said Odette. "There is nothing you can do. The dawn is nearly here, and we will all be swans again."

"I will come back for you," Siegfried cried. "I will find a way to break the spell."

"But go now," Odette sighed. "Only your faithful love can free me from this terror."

All through the next day, the day of the ball, Siegfried was in a dream of love and sorrow. How could he tell his mother that he had found his bride? How could he bring Odette to the palace when Von Rothbart watched and watched her with his amber eyes?

When the ball began and all the princesses were paraded before him, Siegfried hardly noticed them. Then there came a knocking at the gates.

"Lady," said a messenger, kneeling before the Queen, "a knight and his daughter have arrived, and they beg to enter."

"Let them in," said the Queen. "All are welcome at this feast."

The knight was dressed from head to toe in black. Something about his face and the yellowish light that shone from his eyes seemed familiar to Siegfried, but then he caught sight of the knight's daughter and recognized Odette, dressed in glittering black. So happy was he to see his swan-lady again that he forgot every other thought in his head and never considered how his beloved had come to be there, at the palace.

All through his life, the Prince had learned nothing about deception. Even the presence of the black knight did not arouse his suspicions, but the Princess, although she had the body and face of Odette, was none other than Odile, Von Rothbart's daughter. Her father had given her the outward appearance of Odette for one reason and one reason alone: to entrance and delude poor Prince Siegfried, who would thus be tricked into breaking his faith with his true love.

And oh, this Odile, how she danced and turned, and turned and smiled, and how soft were the fires that shone from her eyes, binding Siegfried's heart to her and pushing out of his mind every lingering memory of the real Odette's white dress and her gentle beauty.

They danced together in the light of a thousand candles, but Von Rothbart was always near, weaving stronger and stronger enchantment around them. And as they danced, at the high windows of the Great Hall there was a movement . . . a tremble of white at the glass, but no one saw it, and no one heard the frantic arms beating against the pane.

Von Rothbart spoke at last to Siegfried. "If you will promise to love my daughter forever, she shall be yours."

And the Prince (but where, where had he

seen eyes like that before, and why did the knight's black cloak remind him of wings?) spoke the words Von Rothbart was waiting to hear.

"I will love her, and no one else, for the rest of my days. She is the bride that I have chosen."

A terrible cry came from somewhere high up. Prince Siegfried glanced at the window and saw the bird-shape of Odette pushing at the glass: desperate, despairing.

The instant he looked back at the knight in black, he knew him to be Von Rothbart. And the young woman at his side? How could he, even for a single moment, have thought that she was his princess? And how could he save Odette, now that he had broken his promise to her? Siegfried fled from the Great Hall and ran out into the night. He had to find Odette at the lake and convince her of his love.

At the palace, the guests hurried to leave the ball. The candles flickered and guttered into darkness, and Von Rothbart and his daughter vanished into the night.

Beside the lake, Prince Siegfried found

his princess, weeping and heartbroken. Over and over again he pleaded with her: "I thought that she was you. Oh, the wickedness of that cursed magician!"

"The spell will never be broken for me now," said Odette, "but if I die, then he will die, too. Our lives, his and mine, are twisted into a single thread. What can I live for now?"

"If you are gone," said Siegfried, "life has no meaning for me."

"Then let us die together," said Odette.

At that moment, black wings covered the moon, and Von Rothbart swooped down, desperately trying to pull Odette away from Siegfried.

Siegfried and Von Rothbart struggled and fought, and at last the Prince broke free of the talons and the beak. Taking Odette's hand, he ran towards the lake. A wind had sprung up, whipping the water into waves and whirlpools. The lovers flung themselves in, sinking deeper and deeper until all became silent and calm once again. Von Rothbart flew into the green heart of the forest to die.

Now the swan maidens were free, but they wept bitterly for their princess and her love, together at last.

Listen. These things happened long ago. There is a lake in the forest to this day, but the swans are real swans now. Love, which is stronger than death and lasts forever, has destroyed an evil magic.

On nights when the moon is full, some say they have seen shadows that could be the Princess Odette and her prince, dancing beside the silver water of a lake. A lake they call the Lake of Swans.

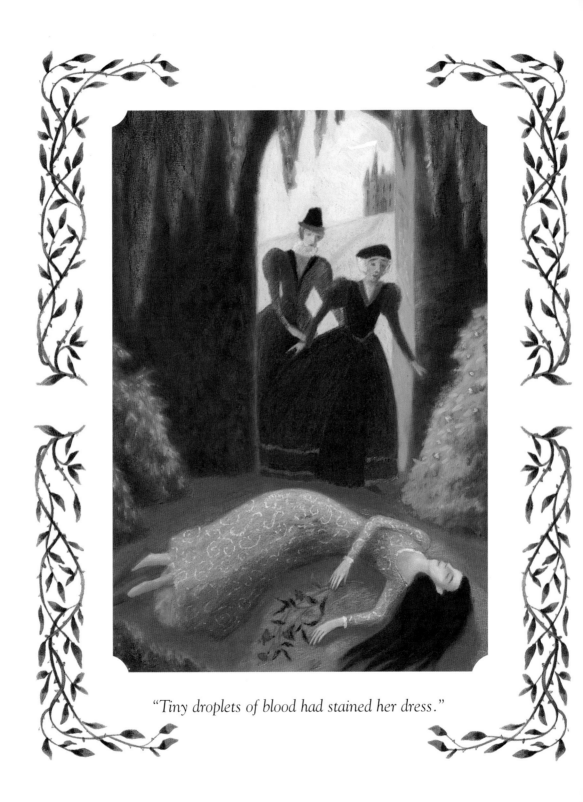

"Tiny droplets of blood had stained her dress."

Sleeping Beauty

MY NAME IS CARABOSSE. People call me all sorts of things. The Bad Fairy, the Wicked Fairy, or the Black Fairy are the most common, but Carabosse is what I prefer. I am old. I am the oldest fairy in the kingdom, and, for this reason alone, you would think that King Florestan and his wife would have seen to it that I received an invitation for what promised to be the most glittering event in the social calendar: the christening of their longed-for baby daughter, Aurora. They thought (and this is their excuse and it is too feeble to be anything but an excuse) that I had retired. Invitation or not, I went anyway.

"No one had seen you," King Florestan told me at the party, "for years and years, and we all thought you had retired, or emigrated."

"Quite the opposite," I said. I was enjoying his embarrassment. In fact, once I had made my entrance, I was determined to enjoy the whole party as much as possible. The best thing of all was the surprise and dismay I caused as I arrived at the door. No one was expecting me.

The entire palace staff had been running around for hours, laying on enough food to feed an army, polishing the wooden floors, dusting down the chandeliers, and wreathing marble columns with garlands of roses. I had seen them in my magic mirror. I'd been watching them for days, and they'd known nothing about it.

At first I thought that I would leave them be to get on with the celebrations, but when I saw them gathering near the cradle, oohing and aahing and behaving in a thoroughly silly fashion, I decided to punish them. I was in a very bad mood that day, I admit. I decided in the blink of an eye that Princess Aurora would have to perish. That would wipe the smiles off their faces, oh, yes indeed! What a lesson it would be for King Florestan and the Queen! How dare they invite the others and leave me out?

By the time I reached the palace (having tossed a few thunderbolts and lightning flashes out of the coach as I passed over the garden, just to announce myself), the other fairies had already given Princess Aurora their gifts. These were exactly the type of thing I had come to expect from my predictable relations: Joy, Beauty, Intelligence, and so forth. Naturally, all the present-giving stopped as soon as I stepped into the room. That was when poor Florestan started mumbling his excuses, but I wasn't interested in listening to him. I went straight to the cradle and said, "I have a gift for the Princess Aurora. Sixteen years of happiness and beauty. And after that, I'm afraid, she will prick her finger on a spindle and drop down dead."

Then I flung myself into my black coach.

"Fly!" I said to the moths that pulled it along. "Fly away. We are not wanted here."

I did feel a great deal better after that but not for long. When I looked into my magic mirror to see what the effect of my announcement was, I discovered that the Lilac Fairy had not yet bestowed her gift. There she was, right before my eyes, busy undoing some of my magic. How dare she!

"Princess Aurora will not die," she was saying, "but sleep for a hundred years until she is woken by a prince's kiss."

I was madder than ever. What good to me was a hundred-year sleep? Kisses from a handsome prince were no part of my plan. I was seething with rage. I went to bed that night vowing to outwit the Lilac Fairy even if it took me sixteen years to do it. How dare she pit her puny powers against me, the wicked fairy Carabosse? I became more determined than ever that the Princess Aurora would not have her life for very long. I would attend to it, even if it were the last thing I ever did.

I, the Lilac Fairy, don't like to speak unkindly of anyone, but I make an exception when it comes to Carabosse. She is so wicked, evil, and ugly that whatever is said about her cannot be too harsh.

Still, the way Carabosse behaved at poor Princess Aurora's christening shocked us all. It was the purest good luck that I had not yet given the baby my gift, and so I was able to soften the ill-wishing just a little.

It's done now. Sixteen years we have waited, and now the waiting is over. Princess Aurora

is asleep in her chamber, with King Florestan and his Queen on comfortable chairs nearby. I have enchanted everyone and every living thing, from the footmen fast asleep in the corridor to the cat curled up by the cold fireside. They will not wake for one hundred years. It is very quiet in the palace now. There will be only dust, gathering on the surfaces of things, because the spiders are asleep and can spin no webs at all. I will raise a forest of thorns and brambles around the building to shield it from sight until the right person comes to break the spell. It is strange to remember that until a few hours ago we had begun to believe that all would be well.

King Florestan banned spindles from his kingdom within minutes of Carabosse's pronouncement. The very next day, there was a bonfire in the market square, and people came from the furthest corners of the

land to throw their spindles into the flames. How the fire leapt and roared, and how we rejoiced to see that everything that could possibly threaten Princess Aurora was reduced to ashes.

Then the years slid by, faster than anyone could have imagined, and, before we knew where we were, it was the Princess's sixteenth birthday. One of my sisters had bestowed on her the gift of beauty, and in her birthday dress she was as lovely as a rosebud. Every rose in the palace garden had bloomed in her honor, and there were garlands everywhere. Four young princes from neighboring territories had come to offer themselves as suitors for her hand, and, although she danced with them in the most delightful way possible, I could see that she would love none of these. Do not ask me how. It is simply my duty as a fairy to know such things, just as I knew that whatever the King and Queen thought, the danger from Carabosse was still something to be reckoned with.

Still, even I, intoxicated with joy and sunshine and the fragrance of the roses, let my guard slip a little. I should have been more careful, more vigilant. I will never cease to blame myself.

A crowd gathered to wish the Princess well. One old lady hobbled up to her with a pretty bunch of flowers. It would have been difficult to refuse such an offering. Princess Aurora took it and thanked the old lady kindly. As the old crone shuffled slowly away into the crowd, something about her seemed to remind me of Carabosse. I would have spoken, but all eyes were on Aurora. She, it seemed, had pricked herself on a thorn. Perhaps the roses in the bouquet had not been carefully trimmed. In any case, she had fainted from the shock, and tiny droplets of blood had stained her dress.

Just then the old lady threw back her hood and cackled, "Oh, look at you all! Fools! Did you think you could defeat me? Idiots! I am Carabosse, and there, in the flowers you will find hidden a spindle. So much for your precious Princess Aurora!"

She flapped her black cloak around her and vanished in a puff of foul-smelling smoke. I took charge at once.

"Bring the Princess to her bedchamber. It has come to pass exactly as I predicted. Let everyone who does not live in the palace leave instantly. We have miracles to perform."

Everyone left the garden. Princess Aurora was carried to her bed, and the rest was easy.

Now they are all sleeping. The forest of briars and thorns is growing even as I speak. Princess Aurora is safe. I, the Lilac Fairy, will guard her for the next hundred years, until the spell is broken. A hundred years is but the twinkling of an eye for me. It will pass.

❧

This has been the strangest day's hunting I've ever had. I set out to find deer, and I found— well, let me tell you the story.

My name is Florimund. I am a prince of the royal blood. We, my companions and I, had decided to explore the hills and valleys beyond our own borders, and that was how we found ourselves in a forest that I had never seen before. There were no trees in this place, only towering brambles and thickets of wild roses. My hunting party grew nervous and begged me to turn back, but I was fascinated by this place.

"You go," I said, "and I will come after you later. I wish to find what is hidden in the heart of this prickly maze."

So they left me, and the silence all around filled my ears. The daylight was fading.

You can imagine how astonished I was, then, when five beautiful ladies suddenly appeared

before me. Their leader, covered in a lilac cloak, stepped forward.

"Do not be afraid, Prince Florimund," she said as she looked into my eyes.

"How do you know my name?" I asked.

"I know many things," she answered. "I know, for instance, who your true love will be. She is closer than you know."

I smiled at this. If she knew everything, how could she not know that I already had my eye on Valentina, the fairest maid in my kingdom?

"I am already in love," I said.

"That is what you think," whispered the lady in the lilac cloak. "But look first at Princess Aurora. Look first, and then tell me that you love another."

I peered through the trees, and there was the most beautiful lady I had ever seen. She glided between the dark branches like a ghost. I moved towards her. She said nothing, only danced with me. Her beauty bewitched me. Then, as quickly as she had appeared, she vanished into the shadows.

"That," said the lady in lilac, "was but a vision of the Princess. The real person is even lovelier. She has been asleep in a palace in the depths of this forest for a hundred years, but she is waiting for someone who loves her to wake her from her long slumber."

"How can I find her?" I cried. "Show me how to find her!"

Because of course the Lilac Fairy was right,

and I had lost my heart entirely.

"Cut down these thorns," she said to me, "and you will find your heart's desire."

She slipped away into the darkness, followed by her companions, and I was all alone. I unsheathed my sword and began to make my way through the tangled branches, cutting and slashing at anything that blocked my path. Thorns tore at the skin of my hands and face. Sharp twigs snatched at my garments. I do not know how long I spent in the forest, but, after what seemed like hours, I caught sight of the white walls of the palace, glimmering in the moonlight.

I should have known that the Forces of Darkness would be lying in wait for me. I was attacked by huge, black moth-shapes and bat-shapes and a hideous crone with a stick and cloak, but I fought on with my sword and drove them back into the shadows.

"Go," I shouted, "you are evil creatures,

and I want nothing to do with you! Nothing is more powerful than my love."

After their shrieks had died away, I made my way into the echoing hall of the palace. Everywhere I looked, people were lying fast asleep, gray under a thick blanket of dust. The Princess, lying on her bed, had been protected by the gauzy bed-curtains. It seemed to me that she had closed her eyes only a moment ago. As soon as I saw her, I knew that I would never love another and that Princess Aurora would be my bride.

I bent over and kissed her. She stirred and opened her eyes. All around us, the palace slowly came to life, but I was unaware of it. I had broken the spell that had bewitched the Princess, but now I was enchanted in turn.

I said, "When I set out for the hunt this morning, I never dreamed that you were what I would find."

Princess Aurora smiled.

❧❀❧

I am Aurora, bride of Prince Florimund, and my wedding party is over. Tomorrow we will set out for his home, and I will see my new kingdom. I will miss my godmothers, the fairies, but I will especially miss the Lilac Fairy. It is thanks to her that Carabosse has at last fled from this land and will worry us no longer. I am grateful to the Lilac Fairy for many things. She looked after me and kept me from the dangers that have beset me since the day I was born. I will miss my parents and my home but will take with me happy memories of my wedding day ball.

"Who would you like," the Lilac Fairy asked, "to dance at your party?"

I was feeling whimsical, I suppose. I said, "I would like Red Riding Hood and the Wolf, Puss-in-Boots and the White Cat, and of course the Bluebird of Happiness."

So my beloved Lilac Fairy worked her magic once again, and there they were, dancing and feasting with all the other guests. Tonight, when I close my eyes, I know that I will wake up in the morning and look into the face of my darling Florimund. The nightmares that filled my head for a hundred years, of black thorns and matted branches, are gone forever, and I will have nothing but sweet dreams from now on.

"Snowflakes, enormous and intricately patterned,
circled all around us."

The Nutcracker

"DREAMS," WHISPERED A DISTANT voice in Clara's ear, "are strange and wonderful things, and the dreams that are dreamed on Christmas Eve are the strangest and most wonderful of all."

Clara opened her eyes. There was the china cabinet and the fireplace, and there in the corner was the Christmas tree. This was most definitely the parlor. Why was she lying on the scratchy plush of the sofa? Why was she not in her own bed, waking up to look for her stocking full of nuts and oranges and twists of golden barley sugar? Clara turned her head and caught sight of the present Dr. Drosselmeyer had given her last night at the party: a wooden nutcracker in the shape of a man. Clara picked him up and cuddled him.

"I love you best, Nutcracker," she said. "Better than my dolls. Better than any game. Better than all my other presents. Do you remember being in my dream last night? Do you remember how it all started? I do."

Clara sat up and gathered the traveling blanket more closely around her shoulders.

"Now I shall tell you the whole story, Nutcracker," Clara said. "Sit comfortably on this cushion, and I'll go right back to the beginning of our party."

The nutcracker said nothing, but he seemed content to listen, so Clara continued. "We always have a party every year on Christmas Eve. Everyone comes to it: grandfathers and grandmothers, aunts, uncles, cousins, friends and neighbors, and Dr. Drosselmeyer. Dr. Drosselmeyer is not a relation, and he's not really a friend, but he always comes to the house on Christmas Eve and brings the most marvelous presents.

"The preparations for the party were almost as exciting as the party itself. All day long, the house had been full of the most mouth-watering smells, and at last Mama began to set out the food on the long table.

"'If you children help with the cakes and sweets,' Mama said, 'there will be none left for the guests! Go instead to fetch your Papa, and decorate the tree.'

"That's what we did, Nutcracker, and, oh, when we'd finished, it was the most beautiful Christmas tree in the whole world. We tied red ribbons on the branches. We hung up painted pine cones and gingerbread cookies frosted in pink and white, and chocolate coins in glittery paper, and Papa found a silver star for the very top of the tree.

"As for the food, you cannot imagine how delicious it was. There were cinnamon cookies and golden shortbread and animals made out of marzipan. There were tiny crystallized fruits, and sugared almonds and salted almonds, and every cake you can think of—ginger cakes and chocolate ones and apple cakes, too—all set out on dainty china plates patterned with flowers, ivy leaves, and trailing ribbons.

"The snow started falling at about four o'clock. Fritz and I watched it from our nursery window as it fell from the dark sky, dancing and whirling as the wind lifted it and tossed it over the rooftops, still falling and falling until everything we could see was covered in white.

"'Just like the frosting on one of the cakes downstairs,' said Fritz.

"When the guests came into the house, snowflakes came in with them: on their hats and capes, on their gloves and boots, and they shook them off, laughing.

"'Dr. Drosselmeyer is here!' Fritz cried, and we both went into the hall to greet him.

"'Good evening, children,' he said in his gravelly voice. 'Come and see who I have brought to your party.'

"Standing behind him in the shadows were a pretty young lady and a young man wearing a harlequin costume.

"'I have taken the liberty of inviting the real Harlequin and Columbine to the festivities.' He put a skinny finger to his lips and whispered to us, 'They are dancing dolls, my dears, nothing more. Life-size and very convincing, but only dolls, when all is said and done. Let us see if we can play a trick on the grown-ups.'

"And they believed him, Nutcracker. Everyone believed him. Harlequin and Columbine danced for all the guests, and everyone thought they were real. When the dance was over and the secret a secret no longer, all the children clustered around the dolls, touching their stiff limbs that only a moment ago had been so full of life and movement.

"Then, Dr. Drosselmeyer gave us our presents. There was a set of soldiers in a wooden box for Fritz, and you were my gift. Oh, I was delighted with you, and everyone admired you greatly. During the parlor games and dances, I never let you out of my sight, and when Fritz and the other boys took you and began cracking nuts with you, why, I almost burst into tears. I did cry when they broke you. Anyone would have. How could they have given you such an enormous nut? It would have broken the strongest nutcracker in the world. Dr. Drosselmeyer noticed my tears.

"'Do not cry, Clara. This is a prince among nutcrackers, and, see, a twist here and a turn there, and he is as good as new.' The doctor's bony, white hands moved so fast that I could not see what he did, but you were completely mended when he returned you to me.

"The end of a party is a sad time, Nutcracker, isn't it? All the candles on the tree had burned out, the gingerbread cookies were all eaten, the table had been cleared, and the white lace cloth folded away. Fritz had put his soldiers back into their box, and I had put you here, on the sofa cushions, to rest until morning. But I couldn't sleep. The thought of you all alone in the dark parlor, kept me awake. I thought: I will creep down and sit on the sofa and keep my Nutcracker company for a while.

"The room was in darkness, except for a faint glow from the embers in the fireplace. I tiptoed to the sofa and sat holding you in my hand. From a long way away, I heard the town clock chiming midnight. Suddenly, the Christmas tree, standing like a shadow in the corner, began to grow. It grew and grew, up and up towards the ceiling with a rustling and creaking and sighing of the branches, and, as it grew, the candles seemed to be alight once again, and, in a few moments, the tree was towering high, high above my head. Now I know I must have been dreaming, but last night I thought there was a special Christmas magic in the air because, all at once, you and I were the same size, and I didn't even stop to consider how strange this was. Then, in the silence of the night, we heard a scratching and a squeaking from behind the Christmas tree.

"'It's the Army of Mice,' you said. Yes, you could speak, and it seemed to me perfectly normal that you should. 'They have come to do battle with the toy soldiers.'

"I could hardly believe my eyes. The mice and the soldiers were enormous. They were the same size as we were, and some were even larger. Our Turkish carpet was turned into a battlefield, with Fritz's army waving their swords and shooting their cannons and marching towards their enemy.

"You, my brave Nutcracker, decided to attack the Mouse King, a fearsome iron-gray creature with glittering red eyes.

"'Nutcracker!' I cried, afraid. 'He will break you . . . I cannot let you be broken again!'

"Suddenly, I was no longer frightened. Instead, I was filled with anger. I took off my slippers and threw them as hard as I could at the Mouse King. Maybe I was helped by Christmas magic once more because both slippers hit the Mouse King right in the face. He was not expecting slippers to come flying through the air, and he ran away squealing into the shadows. His Mouse Army followed him, and soon the soldiers were marching triumphantly back to their box.

"'Thank you, Clara,' you said to me. 'You saved my life.'

"When I turned to look at you, you were no longer made of wood. You had become a real person, living and breathing . . . a handsome prince. Then you took my hand, and we came to sit together on this sofa.

"'Your kindness deserves a reward,' you said. 'Close your eyes, and do not open them until I tell you to.'

"I closed my eyes and felt the sofa moving. It seemed to me that I was flying up and up. I could feel a breeze around us, but I wasn't cold, in spite of being dressed only in my nightgown.

"'Open your eyes, Clara,' you said to me. 'We are in the Land of Snowflakes.'

"There was nothing in the Land of Snowflakes but clear, dark blue everywhere: above, below, and all around us. The sofa was floating on it, through the velvety night.

Snowflakes, enormous and intricately patterned, circled all around us like white moths, floating and drifting, falling and turning.

"'They are dancing, Clara,' you told me. 'They are dancing a Snowflake Waltz.'

"And indeed, when I looked at them more closely, I could see that this was so. Around and around they twirled, like pretty ladies in white dresses, around and around to a music that grew out of the blue night and swelled around us.

"'Come,' you said, when the last snowflake had blown away. 'Now it is time to go somewhere warmer.'

"'Where?' I asked. 'Where are we going now?'

"'To a party in the Land of Sweets.'

"'I have never heard of such a land. When will we reach it?'

"'Soon,' you answered. 'Soon. We must hurry. The Sugar Plum Fairy is waiting for us in her palace.'

"Now, everyone has heard of the witch's house in the story of Hansel and Gretel—the one that was made of things to eat—and I think I was expecting something like that. But I could not have imagined anything half as wonderful as the palace of the Sugar Plum Fairy. It was gigantic and made entirely of pink sugar, spun into domes and turrets and battlements. It was set in a garden full of caramels, marzipan rosebushes, nut cakes, raisins, and pistachios, arranged in tubs and in flowerbeds. The sentries were silver-coated chocolate soldiers.

"We went up the stairs to the front door and stepped inside. The walls of every room in the palace were covered with hard candies like jewels, and the vases were filled with lollipops instead of flowers.

"Then, the Sugar Plum Fairy appeared.

"'Welcome, Prince Nutcracker, and welcome, Clara, to the Land of Sweets. All that is delicious is waiting for you here.'

"Her pink dress caught the light as though she had been sprinkled from head to toe with grains of the finest sugar.

"'When you have eaten and drunk, my

friends,' said the Sugar Plum Fairy, 'we will make music and dance for you.'

"The lamps were lit, and fountains sprang to life. Do you remember all the dances, Nutcracker? There was one in honor of chocolate, with all the dancers in Spanish costumes, then one for coffee, with the dancers dressed in veils and richly patterned Arabian robes. And did you notice the dragons embroidered on the jackets of the Chinese dancers, who represented tea? Oh, they were magnificent. Then came the Russian dancers, with high leather boots and fur hats, and dancers pretending to be reed flutes, and, best of all, was a huge old lady with a wide, wide skirt hiding dozens and dozens of children underneath.

"'Who's that?' I asked, and the Sugar Plum Fairy answered, 'She has many names. Some people call her Mother Ginger or Mother Marshmallow or even the Old Woman who

Lived in a Shoe, but I call her Mère Gigogne.'

"Mère Gigogne and her children stepped aside, the Waltz of the Flowers began, and then, do you remember, Nutcracker? You danced with the Sugar Plum Fairy. To me it seemed as though her feet never touched the ground. You looked so beautiful, both of you. I have never seen a lovelier sight.

"There's always a dance at the end of every party, but in the Land of Sweets the last waltz was like a kaleidoscope of sparkling colors, turning and turning.

"After the party was over, you and I, Nutcracker, went back into the garden of the palace and sat down again on our sofa.

"'It is time for you to leave us,' said the Sugar Plum Fairy as she bent to kiss me goodbye. 'Take a little rose from this marzipan rosebush.' She put into my hand a pink flower nestling among leaves of green angelica.

"'Thank you,' I said. 'It has been like a dream.'

"'Dreams,' said the Sugar Plum Fairy, 'are strange and wonderful things, and the dreams that are dreamed on Christmas Eve are the strangest and most wonderful of all.'

"That's what she said to me, Nutcracker. Then I woke up. There was a blanket covering me. Mama must have come in and found me asleep. Wasn't that a sweet dream, Nutcracker?"

Clara listened for the nutcracker's answer, but he only smiled and said nothing.

Unnoticed under the sofa, a small, pink marzipan rose, nestling among green angelica leaves, lay where it had fallen.

"*Prince Ivan followed the Firebird, and, as she fluttered to
the ground, he stalked her as silently as any cat.*"

The Firebird

LONG, LONG AGO AND far, far away over the gray, looming mountains, in a place where the trees grow tall and dark and the wolves still howl by moonlight, there lived (so the old stories tell us) a sorcerer whose name was Kostchei.

His palace was set in a garden filled with magic, and travelers told of an orchard where golden apples grew on an enchanted tree. Kostchei was immortal, as long as his soul was kept separate from his body. So he kept it locked up in an egg encrusted with moonstones and rubies, and he kept this egg well hidden—for no one could kill him if his soul was safely guarded.

Maybe his heart also lay in that same egg because he was by all accounts the most heartless sorcerer you could ever wish to meet. Trespassers in his garden were turned to stone or into frog-like, hopping creatures or into hideous monsters with dark patches on what used to be their faces. Some of his enemies he had bewitched so that they did only his bidding. They forgot who they had been, and where they had come from, and these poor, wretched things moved through Kostchei's palace and the grounds beyond like clockwork dolls. But it was the Princess Tsarevna and her attendant maidens who gave Kostchei the most pleasure. After all, it was not every sorcerer who had such beauty under his control.

And what did he look like, this Kostchei? Like your very worst nightmares, my children: dark as shadows, tall as towers, and pale as dead men's bones. As for his hands . . . his nails were as long and silvery as knives, and his voice was as cold as the winds blown down from the Arctic Circle.

Do you feel cold, my children? Gather around the hearth, close to me, and I will tell you how the evil Kostchei was defeated. Look into the fire, and tell me what you see. Scarlet and sparkling gold, yes indeed. Something that leaps and glows and dances like a living creature made of light and heat: the fire itself. But look closer. See how the shapes of the flames change as you watch them. If you look very hard you will see a bird with burning feathers, there, in the very heart of the brightest coals. That is the Firebird, the most beautiful bird in all the world.

But how could a bird, even a bird whose beauty shines like a flame, overcome the wicked Kostchei and defeat his evil plans? Listen carefully, my children, and I will tell you exactly what happened.

One evening, then, just as the sun was setting behind the mountains to the west, Prince Ivan was wandering through the forest, trying to find his way home. All at once, he saw a wall, with apple branches nodding over it.

"Some great nobleman obviously lives here," Prince Ivan said to himself. "He is sure to tell me where I am and how I may find my way home. I will climb the wall and ask for help.'

Just as Prince Ivan was climbing over the wall into Kostchei's garden, he caught sight of the Firebird, flying over the orchard. Her tail feathers streamed behind her as she flew, and she lit up the darkening branches with her brilliance as she passed over them. Prince Ivan immediately put an arrow to his bow and took aim but found himself powerless to kill the beautiful creature. "I cannot justify destroying such a magnificent bird," he thought, "and yet how wonderful it would be to capture her. I would look after her well and feast my eyes on her beauty forever."

Prince Ivan followed the Firebird, and, as she fluttered to the ground, he stalked her as silently as any cat. At last, he caught her. The poor Firebird struggled in his arms, and she cried, "Let me go, Prince Ivan. Have pity on me. I know you mean me no harm, but I will die if I am caged. How will I spread my wings?"

Prince Ivan looked at the Firebird's wings, at her gold and scarlet plumage flickering like small flames, and said, "You are right, beautiful bird. I will set you free to fly and light up the night with your radiance."

The Firebird rearranged her feathers. "I will go now, Prince Ivan, but, before I do, here is my gift to you, to thank you for your kindness. It is one of my feathers, and if ever you feel that I can help you, hold it in your hand and say these words:

Firebird, hear me.

Firebird, help me.

Firebird, appear to me.

Firebird, draw near to me.

and immediately I will be at your side."

"Thank you," said Prince Ivan, putting the feather carefully into his vest pocket. Secretly, he wondered how a mere bird, however magnificent, could possibly help a royal prince armed with the sharpest of swords, but he was a polite young man who knew his manners, and so he said nothing. The Firebird rose above the tree in a bright fluttering of feathers, flew into the sky, and disappeared.

"I must find my way out of here," said the Prince to himself, but the very next instant he saw, almost floating in the darkness between the tree trunks, a line of young maidens dressed in white. The loveliest of the maidens came first and led her companions in a dance around a tree that Prince Ivan had not noticed before. Every apple on this tree was made of gold, and the maidens picked one of the shining fruits and tossed it in the air as though it were a ball.

Prince Ivan stepped forward out of the shadows and said to the most beautiful of the dancers, "My name is Prince Ivan, and I am lost in these woods. Until I saw you, I counted that as my misfortune, but now that I have seen you, I bless the fate that has brought me here to your side. Tell me your name, for I will love you till the day I die."

The lady shook her head. "You must go at once. You must not love me—for nothing will come of it. I am the Princess Tsarevna and these are my ladies, and we are all prisoners of the sorcerer Kostchei. This is his enchanted garden. Oh, flee, Prince Ivan, flee at once! If he catches you, he will turn you to stone."

Prince Ivan said, "Only because you beg me, Tsarevna, will I flee, but I will return to rescue you and your maidens."

"Shh, do not speak," cried Tsarevna. "You must leave now. Can't you hear the trumpets? He is coming . . . oh, hurry, hurry!"

Prince Ivan turned and ran, but out of the darkness a huge, wrought-iron gate appeared and blocked his path.

"I cannot escape!" he called out to the Princess. "The gates are locked. I am doomed, for I can see him approaching."

Just then, the metal gates swung open and Kostchei swept into his orchard wrapped in his long, black cloak. Behind him followed his monstrous army.

Can you picture them, my children? Half-animal, half-human, furry, spotted, crawling, leaping—all the creatures unlucky enough to have fallen under Kostchei's spell were forming a circle around Prince Ivan.

Kostchei spoke, and his voice was like cracking ice, and the silver daggers of his fingernails sliced up the air.

"Who is this who dares invade the silence of my orchard?"

"My name is Ivan," said the Prince, "and I am not afraid of you, Kostchei."

A great murmuring and sighing rose from Kostchei's creatures, but, when their master spoke, they fell silent.

"Look at this world," Kostchei said, "because soon you will be turned to stone, and others will look upon you. What a fine statue Your Highness will make!"

All at once, Prince Ivan remembered the feather that the Firebird had given him. He pulled it out of his vest pocket and waved it high in the air, crying:

Firebird, hear me.

Firebird, help me.

Firebird, appear to me.

Firebird, draw near to me.

Lightning zigzagged across the night sky, and there before him was the Firebird herself. Her fiery plumage dazzled the sorcerer, and he shrank away from her.

She shook her feathers and spoke to Kostchei's dreadful followers, "You wish to rejoice at Prince Ivan's destruction, and to dance is to rejoice. I say you will dance, every one of you, until you can dance no more. Now begin."

Kostchei was completely powerless— don't you know, my children, that heat can melt even the coldest ice? So it is that Goodness will always have dominion over Evil, and, when Goodness is ablaze, then Darkness shrinks before it and soon vanishes altogether.

The monstrous horde began to dance. They could not stop themselves. Their legs and arms whirled them around and around, faster and faster, until they could no longer stand upright. At last, they fell exhausted to the ground.

"You have danced until you have dropped," said the Firebird, "and now you will sleep."

She rustled her beautiful golden wings in a soothing lullaby and everyone slept. Everyone, that is, except for Prince Ivan and the wicked Kostchei.

"I am immortal!" he shrieked. "You may use your magic on them but never on me."

The Firebird laughed. "Prince Ivan, you must now act quickly. Break the egg that holds the immortal soul of this wicked enchanter. Take it from its hiding place in the dark hollow of that tree, and break it into a thousand fragments."

"Oh, no, no!" screamed Kostchei, flapping his black cloak around him. "Not my soul . . . leave me my soul. Oh, I will die if the egg is broken!"

It was too late; Prince Ivan had found the egg, encrusted with rubies and moonstones, and thrown it to the ground with all his strength. As it cracked, the heavens were filled with thunder that could have been Kostchei roaring in the agony of his death. Utter darkness fell from the sky and utter silence. Then a pale golden light began to creep over the horizon. Dawn was breaking, and Prince Ivan shook his head in wonder. Where were Kostchei's monsters and creatures?

What had become of Tsarevna and her maidens? The forest, the orchard, the wall, and the gate: everything had vanished, and of the Firebird not so much as a single feather remained.

Prince Ivan was in the hall of a palace, surrounded by courtiers and finely dressed ladies. Trumpets sounded, and, then, in a long line, just as they had appeared in Kostchei's garden, his beloved and her ladies came into the hall. Prince Ivan took Tsarevna's hand, and one of the courtiers said, "You have released us all from the darkness of Kostchei's enchantment. Stay and be our King and the Princess Tsarevna will be Queen."

Thus it was that Evil was banished from the land, and a new Tsar and Tsarina came to the throne of Russia. Prince Ivan never forgot what he owed to the Firebird. That is why, my children, every winter, when the days grow shorter and the nights longer, we spend many hours gazing into the leaping flames. We are hoping for a glimpse of her glossy wings, flickering among the black coals. And, if we are lucky, just for a second we may see the power and beauty of the Firebird.

*About
the Ballets*

GISELLE WAS FIRST PERFORMED at the Paris Opéra in 1841. It was choreographed by Jean Coralli for the ballerina Carlotta Grisi. The French poet, Théophile Gautier, devised the story from a German original by fellow poet Heinrich Heine. The music is by Adolphe Adam. Giselle is a wonderful part for any female dancer, a part she dreams of throughout her long and difficult training.

Of all the arts, ballet is probably the most demanding. Not everyone has the right frame, strength or temperament to be trained as a dancer. Those who do must have a passion for ballet and the discipline that goes with it.

All dancers have to devote themselves to their training, which begins in early childhood and never ends. Even the greatest principal dancers have to attend class daily, doing many of the same exercises as the youngest beginner, in order to maintain the strength and suppleness of their bodies. Dancers must try to avoid injury, and this is why the daily class is so important: it is much easier to damage limbs that have not been thoroughly stretched and warmed up.

The names given to the steps and exercises are in French, and, wherever you learn to dance, you will use the same terms. Five foot positions must be learned, and each jump, turn, and lift has its own name that is known to every dancer.

It used to be thought unmanly for boys to show an interest in ballet dancing, but anyone who sees a video of Irek Mukhamedov or Tetsuya Kumakawa will know that a dancer requires all the power and energy we associate with the strongest athletes.

Many of the greatest dancers eventually become teachers. In this way, they pass on steps and stylistic techniques which would otherwise disappear, and the dancers of today become part of a long tradition of beauty and precision.

COPPÉLIA (music by Léo Delibes and choreography by Arthur Saint-Léon) was first produced in 1870. The original story is by E.T.A. Hoffmann. He also wrote the story which is the basis for *The Nutcracker*.

The ballet, like theater, opera, and movies, is an art form that involves a great number of people. There are composers and musicians, and many dancers. Just as with movies, however, many people are attracted to the ballet because of its stars. Everyone knows the names of Pavlova and Nijinsky, of Nureyev and Fonteyn. These are all dancers from the past, but they are more than dancers; they are stars.

The stars of today (Darcey Bussell, Viviana Durante, Sylvie Guillem) draw the crowds to the ballet all over the world, dancing in New York one week and Sydney the next.

Film has made it possible for us to see stars from the past. There is some flickering footage of Anna Pavlova dancing *The Dying Swan* which is very moving and beautiful. Looking at it, we understand why audiences from Paris to Peru flocked to see her.

Sometimes a very young dancer can be picked out by a dance master or choreographer for a leading role very early in his or her career. This happened to Sylvie Guillem, who was chosen by Nureyev when he was Artistic Director of the Paris Opéra to be Cinderella when she was only seventeen. Alicia Markova, one of the youngest of all stars, joined the Diaghilev Ballet in 1925 at the age of fourteen and appeared as Odette in *Swan Lake* the same year.

No one knows exactly what it is that makes a star. It's much more than grace or beauty. They are the performers who simply seem to embody something of the magic of the ballet.

SWAN LAKE WAS FIRST produced in 1877. The music was by Tchaikovsky, and the production was a failure. In 1894, after the composer's death, the ballet was revived with new choreography by Marius Petipa and was a great success. Today, it is probably the best-known of all ballets.

Although you will often hear of daring experiments with plays—of Hamlet set in a prison, or Romeo and Juliet on the streets of New York—it is rarer for a ballet to be staged in a non traditional way, although this is sometimes done.

There are, of course, many modern ballets which take place not in a kind of fairyland but in the real, recognizable world. *The Judas Tree*, for instance, takes place on a construction site.

It is possible for classical ballets to be staged in different kinds of spaces: in the round, in school auditoriums, in tents, and so forth. But ballet companies have their homes for the most part in beautiful theaters that date back to the last century or earlier.

The Paris Opéra, right in the heart of the city, is a magnificent building. Inside, there are wide staircases, marble columns, and all the glitter and glamour that we have come to associate with ballet. The Maryinski Theater in St. Petersburg, the Bolshoi Theater in Moscow, and Covent Garden in London are all dazzling, with their velvet curtains and chandeliers and plush, padded boxes. There is no rule that says you have to dress up to go to the ballet, but when the theater is so sumptuous, part of the fun is dressing up in your best clothes especially for the occasion.

The magic we see on stage is a combination of many elements. As the auditorium grows dark and the orchestra starts to play, we step into the dancers' world of music, drama, and bright lights.

THE SLEEPING BEAUTY WAS first put on in 1890. The music was by Tchaikovsky and the choreography by Marius Petipa. The fairy tale is a very ancient one, but it was first written down in the eighteenth century by a Frenchman named Charles Perrault.

The choreographer of a ballet decides which steps should be danced on stage and in which order. They are responsible for the overall pattern of the ballet and for every individual step taken by each member of the cast.

There have been many famous choreographers. The work of Petipa, Nijinsky, and Fokine can still be seen today, as their ideas have passed down to a new generation of choreographers who have danced the steps themselves. Modern choreographers like to add something of their own and make changes to well-known works, but you can still see ballets danced today that are just like those of a century ago.

Swan Lake, *The Sleeping Beauty*, and *La Bayadère* are all the creations of Marius Petipa, the most famous choreographer of the Imperial Russian period. He worked very closely with Tchaikovsky on *The Nutcracker* but was prevented from choreographing this ballet because of illness.

You could say that the choreography is an extension of the music, the spirit of the music made visible. If the choreographer sees qualities in a dancer that they would like to develop and emphasize, they can create a whole ballet around that specific person's skills.

Choreographers have to keep in their heads not only each single dancer's movements, but also the way in which a whole company of people uses the stage and fills it with constantly changing patterns. By the time we see the ballet, the dancers and their movements seem to have grown naturally from the music.

THE NUTCRACKER WAS PERFORMED for the first time in 1892. It was choreographed first by Petipa and then by Lev Ivanov after Petipa got sick. The story is by Hoffmann, and the music was the last great ballet score written by Tchaikovsky before his death.

You can dance to any music as long as it has a strong, definite rhythm. There have been ballets set to jazz, rock'n'roll, and many classical pieces that were not written especially for the dance. For example, the ballet *Les Sylphides* can also be called *Chopiniana* because Fokine choreographed it as a physical embodiment of the music of Chopin.

Sometimes the composer tries to express a story or a scene that the choreographer has visualized. Tchaikovsky was supremely skilled at doing this, and so was Stravinsky, who wrote the score for *The Firebird*. Prokofiev is another famous composer, whose *Romeo and Juliet* is still performed by every major ballet company. There is a beautiful version of it on video, danced by Rudolf Nureyev and Margot Fonteyn.

Music written for ballet has to do some of the same things as movie music. It has to help convey a certain atmosphere. It tells us the mood we are supposed to be in. Some ballet music is so well-known that we associate it with other things. Advertisers often use ballet music in their jingles, and ballet music is frequently used as the background sound when we are put on hold, or standing in an elevator. It comes as a delightful surprise when you see your first ballet and a melody that you already recognize is suddenly transformed by being part of a beautiful whole.

Music does far more than provide a background for the dancing. It is the transformation of what the composer has written into what we hear that casts the first spell. The music is where the magic begins.

THE FIREBIRD WAS FIRST produced in 1910 as part of Diaghilev's second season in Paris. The story is an old Russian legend. The choreography is by Fokine, and the music was Stravinsky's first ballet score. The set and costumes were by Golovin, and the costumes of the Firebird and the Princess were designed by Bakst.

The look of a ballet depends on the designers of both the sets and costumes. Modern ballets can take place on bare stages with the dancers dressed in leotards, but the Romantic ballets and works such as *The Firebird* rely greatly on the work of the designers. We expect the lake in *Swan Lake* to be eerily beautiful in the moonlight, and the Wilis in *Giselle* to be dressed in floating garments that suggest the mistiness of the swamp and their own ghostly nature. Dancers need to be able to move their bodies freely. That is why the women's costumes are made from gauzy, light materials.

Every dancer needs to learn to sew well enough to be able to do emergency repairs and attach the ribbons to their *pointe* shoes. Because ballet shoes are made of delicate satin, dancers wear out many pairs. Sometimes a principal will use three or four pairs in one evening.

Some ballets allow set designers to try all kinds of spectacular effects. Many famous artists like Picasso and Hockney have designed for the stage. Bakst's designs for *Schéhérazade* in 1910 created a sensation because he used explosive colors in a way no one had seen before.

Whenever you watch a ballet, the everyday world disappears and you become part of another universe, where dancers leap and turn, and where strange and beautiful stories unfold, before the velvet curtains close and the music ends.